J595.44 WHE
Wheeler, Jill C., 1964-
Crab spiders /

7/08

CR

No LONGER THE PROPERTY OF
WICHITA PUBLIC LIBRARY

SPIDERS SET II

CRAB SPIDERS

Jill C. Wheeler
ABDO Publishing Company

visit us at
www.abdopub.com

Published by ABDO Publishing Company, 4940 Viking Drive, Edina, Minnesota 55435.
Copyright © 2006 by Abdo Consulting Group, Inc. International copyrights reserved in all
countries. No part of this book may be reproduced in any form without written permission from
the publisher. The Checkerboard Library™ is a trademark and logo of ABDO Publishing
Company.

Printed in the United States.

Cover Photo: Peter Arnold
Interior Photos: Animals Animals pp. 7, 18; Corbis pp. 5, 6, 9, 13; Peter Arnold pp. 14-15, 17;
    Visuals Unlimited pp. 11, 19, 21

Series Coordinator: Stephanie Hedlund
Editors: Stephanie Hedlund, Megan Murphy
Art Direction: Neil Klinepier

Library of Congress Cataloging-in-Publication Data

Wheeler, Jill C., 1964-
    Crab spiders / Jill C. Wheeler.
        p. cm. -- (Spiders. Set II)
    ISBN 1-59679-292-2
    1. Crab spiders--Juvenile literature. I. Title.

    QL458.4.W45 2005
    595.4'4--dc22

                                                                2005043277

CONTENTS

CRAB SPIDERS 4

SIZES 6

SHAPES 8

COLORS 10

WHERE THEY LIVE 12

SENSES 14

DEFENSE 16

FOOD 18

BABIES 20

GLOSSARY 22

WEB SITES 23

INDEX 24

CRAB SPIDERS

All spiders are **arachnids**. Scorpions, ticks, and mites are arachnids, too. All arachnids have two body parts and eight legs. They are also all **arthropods**. This means their skeletons are on the outside of their bodies.

There are about 100 **families** of spiders. Several of these families are types of crab spiders. The most common crab spider family is the Thomisidae family.

There are 3,000 different species of crab spiders. So, they can be found all over the world. In fact, North America alone has more than 200 species of crab spiders.

The only places crab spiders cannot live are the driest deserts and highest mountain tops. That is because there is no food for them to eat in those places.

Opposite page: *Crab spiders eat mites, flies, mosquitoes, and other insect pests. This makes them a big help to humans.*

Sizes

Crab spiders come in several different sizes. The smallest species are only about 5/32 of an inch (4 mm) long. The largest species are about one inch (2.5 cm) in length. Female crab spiders are usually much bigger than males.

All spiders have eight legs. The crab spider's four front legs are longer than the four rear legs. Crab spiders often hold these long front legs up and apart when hunting. This way they are ready to grab their prey. The spider uses its smaller rear legs to move around.

This crab spider is ready to catch its prey.

The giant crab spider is in the family Sparassidae.

SHAPES

All spiders have two body parts. The head and **thorax** make up the front body part. This is also called the **cephalothorax**. The wide, rear body part is called the abdomen.

Spiders share other common **traits**, too. They all have two **pedipalps**, which they use to capture prey. Spiders also have two **chelicerae**, which they use for killing and eating their meals.

Crab spiders got their name from the way they look. Like crabs, their bodies are short, wide, and flat. The back portion of the crab spider's abdomen is wider than the front. These spiders can walk sideways like crabs. They move forward and backward, too.

The Body Parts of a Crab Spider

Cephalothorax

Abdomen

Leg

Pedipalp

Chelicera

COLORS

Crab spiders vary in color. They are often colored to match their **environment**. Sometimes, males and females of the same species are different colors.

Many crab spiders live in gardens and meadows. There, they sit on plants and flowers to wait for insects. Some crab spiders are white, yellow, or bright pink to match the flowers they sit on. These colorful species are also called flower spiders.

Other crab spiders are dark with gray and brown patterns. They can look like tree bark or dry, wrinkled leaves. Some species of crab spiders look like fruit, such as the goldenrod spider. These spiders often hide in banana bunches.

Some crab spiders can change color to match their environment. A white spider may move from a white flower to a yellow one. Then, it will start to turn yellow. A complete color change takes several days.

The use of color to blend in with the environment is called camouflage.

WHERE THEY LIVE

Crab spiders are a little different from most other spiders. They do not spin webs. Instead, crab spiders are free-living spiders. They live on the ground, on trees, or on plants.

Crab spiders live wherever they can find food. Some species find homes on plants **pollinated** by bees and other tasty bugs. Other species will roam around looking for prey. Crab spiders tend to live and hunt alone.

Some crab spiders do not move around very much at all. They may stay in exactly the same place for several days. This makes them harder to see. When crab spiders are active, they move more during the day than at night.

Sometimes crab spiders don't have to be the same color as their surroundings. As long as they sit still, birds and other predators won't realize they are there.

SENSES

All crab spiders in the Thomisidae **family** have eight eyes. The eyes are on raised bumps on the **cephalothorax**. This lets the spider see in all directions.

But, crab spiders do not have very good eyesight. They can see movement, but little else. They have to rely on sensing vibrations instead.

Crab spiders sense vibrations through thousands of tiny hairs on their bodies and legs. The hairs move when the air near them moves. Then, the spider knows something is nearby.

Opposite page: The two center eyes in the front row are the crab spider's main eyes. The other six eyes are secondary eyes that are mostly for sensing movement.

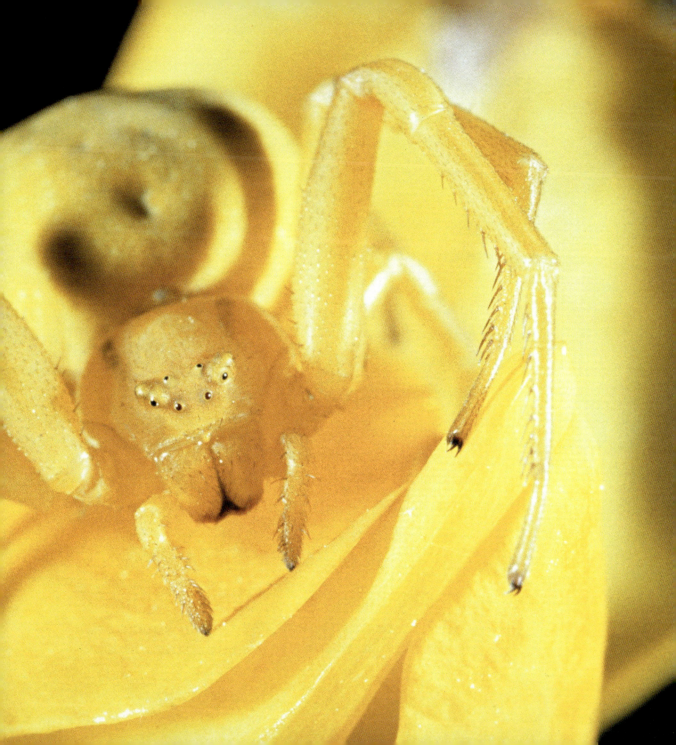

DEFENSE

Crab spiders like to eat bugs. Yet, many other creatures like to eat crab spiders. Wasps, ants, birds, lizards, and some other spiders think crab spiders are tasty.

Crab spiders use camouflage to hide from their enemies. Sitting still also helps them stay hidden. Hiding is the crab spider's first form of defense. Few people ever see crab spiders unless they are really looking for them.

Their second form of defense is to bite their enemies. But the crab spider's **venom** really only works against other **invertebrates**. Their venom does not usually hurt vertebrates. So, it is rare for a human to have a bad reaction to a crab spider's bite.

Opposite page: *This crab spider uses camouflage to look like a sunflower.*

FOOD

Crab spiders feast on bugs such as bees and butterflies. These insects are often attracted to the same plants and flowers as crab spiders.

Crab spiders are good hunters. They **ambush** their prey. Typically, a crab spider will wait until something comes nearby. Then it will grab its prey with its long front legs.

Once the prey is caught, the spider bites the insect with its fangs. The fangs are located on the **chelicerae**. The fangs **inject**

Ants are some of the pest insects that crab spiders eat.

deadly **venom** into the insect. The venom quickly makes the insect unable to move.

Crab spiders do not chew their food. Instead, they **inject digestive** juices into their prey. This turns the prey's insides to mush. The spider then slowly sucks out the mush.

Despite their small size, crab spiders have big appetites. These spiders can be found eating bugs much larger than they are.

BABIES

Crab spiders have interesting mating habits. Males are much smaller than females. So, the male will often wrap the female in silk during mating. That way she cannot bite him.

After mating, the female makes an egg sac of silk. She carefully puts her eggs in this sac. The sac may be placed out in the open, on the grass, or on a plant.

The spider then sits on the egg sac to protect it. She will stay that way until the eggs hatch. The mother crab spider usually starves to death before the eggs can hatch. Her babies, called spiderlings, crawl out of the egg sac about three weeks later.

Like most young spiders, these colorless crab spiderlings climb as high as they can go. Each spins a thin strand of silk and waits for a breeze. The breeze catches the silk and carries the spiderling away. This is called ballooning.

Even if they do not spin webs, all spiders have spinnerets that make silk. The silk is used for mating, making egg sacs, and ballooning.

Spiderlings shed their skeletons several times as they grow. This is called molting. Most spiders molt up to 14 times before they are adults. Crab spiders molt several times during their one-year life span.

GLOSSARY

ambush - a surprise attack from a hidden position.

arachnid (uh-RAK-nuhd) - an order of animals with two body parts and eight legs.

arthropod - a member of the phylum Arthropoda with an exterior skeleton.

cephalothorax (seh-fuh-luh-THAWR-aks) - the front body part of an arachnid that has the head and thorax.

chelicera (kih-LIH-suh-ruh) - either of the leglike organs of a spider that has a fang attached to it.

digestive - of or relating to the breakdown of food into substances small enough for the body to absorb.

environment - all the surroundings that affect the growth and well-being of a living thing.

family - a group that scientists use to classify similar plants or animals. It ranks above a genus and below an order.

inject - to forcefully introduce a fluid into the body, usually with a needle or something sharp.

invertebrate (ihn-VUHR-tuh-bruht) - an animal without a backbone. A vertebrate has a spine.

pedipalp (PEH-duh-palp) - either of the leglike organs of a spider that are used to sense motion and catch prey.

pollinate - when birds and insects transfer pollen from one flower or plant to another.

thorax - part of the front body of an arachnid that contains the head and lungs.

trait - a quality that distinguishes one person or group from another.

venom - a poison produced by some animals and insects. It usually enters a victim through a bite or sting.

WEB SITES

To learn more about crab spiders, visit ABDO Publishing Company on the World Wide Web at **www.abdopub.com**. Web sites about these spiders are featured on our Book Links page. These links are routinely monitored and updated to provide the most current information available.

INDEX

A

abdomen 8
arthropods 4

B

ballooning 20

C

camouflage 10, 16
cephalothorax 8, 14
chelicerae 8, 18
color 10

D

defense 10, 16

E

egg sac 20
eyes 14

F

families 4, 14

flower spiders 10
food 4, 6, 8, 10, 12,
    16, 18, 19

G

goldenrod spiders 10

H

homes 10, 12
hunting 6, 12, 18

L

legs 4, 6, 14, 18
life span 21

M

mating 20
mites 4
molting 21

N

North America 4

P

pedipalps 8
predators 16

S

scorpions 4
senses 14
silk 20
size 6, 8, 20, 21
skeletons 4, 21
species 4, 6, 10, 12
spiderlings 20, 21

T

Thomisidae 4, 14
ticks 4

V

venom 16, 19
vibrations 14

W

webs 12

24